THE JUNGLE BOOK

Library of Congress Cataloging-in-Publication Data

Ashachik, Diane M., (date)
    The jungle book / by Rudyard Kipling: retold by Diane M. Ashachik;
illustrated by Holly Hannon.
        p.   cm.—(Troll illustrated classics)
    Summary: Presents the adventures of Mowgli, a boy reared by a pack
of wolves and the wild animals of the jungle.
    ISBN 0-8167-2868-2 (lib. bdg.)   ISBN 0-8167-2869-0 (pbk.)
    [1. Jungles—Fiction.   2. Animals—Fiction.   3. India—Fiction.]
I. Hannon, Holly, ill. II. Kipling, Rudyard, 1865-1936. Jungle
book. III. Title.
PZ7.A798Ju 1993
[Fic]—dc20   92-5806

THE JUNGLE BOOK

RUDYARD KIPLING

Retold by
Diane Ashachik

Illustrated by
Holly Hannon

Troll Associates

It was seven o'clock on a warm evening in India's Seeonee hills when Father Wolf woke from his day's rest. With a yawn, he spread his paws to get rid of the sleepy feeling in their tips. Mother Wolf lay nearby with her big gray nose across her four tumbling, squealing cubs.

Father Wolf walked to the mouth of their cave and listened. Below in the valley he heard the dry, snarly, singsong whine of a tiger on the prowl.

"Shere Khan. That fool!" said Father Wolf. "To begin a night's work with all that noise!"

"Shere Khan has shifted his hunting grounds?" asked Mother Wolf. "By the Law of the Jungle he has no right to come here without warning."

Shere Khan was the tiger who lived near the Waingunga River, twenty miles away. Lame in one foot since birth, Shere Khan usually hunted only cattle. That had made the Waingunga villagers angry with him, so he had decided to move to new territory. It was bad news for the wolves.

"Now he'll make *our* villagers angry," said Mother Wolf softly. "They'll scour the jungle for him, with guns and rockets and torches. We and our children will have to run when the grass is set alight."

Then there was a howl—an untigerish howl—from Shere Khan in the valley below. "He has missed," said Mother Wolf. "What happened?"

Father Wolf took a few steps forward. "The fool had no more sense than to jump at a woodcutter's campfire. He's burned his feet," he said with a grunt.

"There's something coming up the hill," whispered Mother Wolf, twitching one ear. "Get ready."

Father Wolf dropped down on his haunches, ready to defend his family. He sprang before he saw what he was jumping at, then tried to stop himself. The result was that he shot straight up into the air, landing almost where he left the ground. Directly in front of him stood a small boy barely old enough to walk.

"Man!" Father Wolf snapped. "A man's cub. Look!"

"I've never seen one before," said Mother Wolf. "Bring him here."

Father Wolf gently picked up the child and laid him among the cubs.

"How little! And—how bold!" said Mother Wolf. The baby was pushing his way between the cubs to get close to her warm fur. "I could kill him with a touch of my foot. But see, he looks up and is not afraid."

Father Wolf sniffed the child cautiously. "He looks just like a little frog."

"And that's what I'll call him," said Mother Wolf thoughtfully. "Mowgli—my little frog."

"Then you intend to keep him?" Father Wolf asked with some surprise.

Suddenly, the moonlight was blocked out of the mouth of the cave. The great square head and shoulders of a tiger crowded into the narrow entrance.

"Shere Khan does us great honor," said Father Wolf, but his eyes were angry. "What does Shere Khan need?"

"My dinner," growled the tiger. "A man's cub ran this way. Its parents have run off. Give it to me."

"The Wolves are a free people," said Father Wolf. "We take orders from the Head of the Pack. The man's cub is ours to keep or to kill, as we choose."

"As you choose?" Shere Khan roared. "It is *I*, Shere Khan, who speaks!"

"And it is *I*, Raksha, who answers," Mother Wolf snarled, springing forward. Her eyes glittered like two moons in the darkness. "The man's cub is mine. He shall not be killed. He shall live to run with the Pack. And in the end, you hunter of little hairless cubs, he shall hunt *you*!"

Shere Khan might have faced Father Wolf alone. But he knew he could not stand up against them both in the narrow cave. He backed out, growling. "Each dog barks in his own yard," he shouted when he was clear of the entrance. "We'll see what the Pack will say at the next Council meeting."

The Law of the Jungle states that any wolf may, when he marries, withdraw from the Pack he belongs to. But when his cubs are old enough to stand on their feet, he must bring them to the Pack Council.

So at the next full moon, Father Wolf rounded up his family and took them to Council Rock. Forty or more wolves were already there when they arrived. An enormous gray wolf stretched full length on one rock. It was Akela, the Lone Wolf, who led all the Pack because of his strength and cunning. ''Look well, O Wolves! You know the Law,'' he cried.

Dozens of cubs tumbled over one another in the circle where their mothers and fathers sat. Now and then, a senior wolf would go quietly up to a cub to look at it carefully. Sometimes a mother would push her cub far out into the moonlight. No wolf wanted her cub to be overlooked.

At last, Mother Wolf pushed Mowgli into the center. He laughed and played with some pebbles that glistened in the moonlight. Akela never raised his head from his paws, but went on with his cry, ''Look well! You know the Law.''

A muffled roar came up from behind the rocks: "The cub is mine." It was the voice of Shere Khan.

"Give him to me," said the tiger, stepping out into the circle. "What have the Free People to do with a man's cub?"

Akela didn't even twitch his ears. "Look well, O Wolves," he repeated. "What have the Free People to do with the orders of anyone but the Free People? Look well!"

There was a chorus of deep growls, and a young wolf stepped forward. "What *have* the Free People to do with a man's cub?" he asked.

Now, the Law of the Jungle is clear about what happens if there is any disagreement about accepting a cub. The cub must be spoken for by at least two members who are not its father and mother.

"Who speaks for this cub?" asked Akela.

There was no answer.

Then a deep, rumbling voice arose from the side of the crowd. "I speak for him," said an enormous brown bear, rising up on his hindquarters. It was Baloo, teacher of the Law of the Jungle. He was the only other creature allowed at the Pack Council. He could come and go as he pleased because he ate only nuts and roots and honey.

"There is no harm in a man's cub," Baloo said. "I have no gift of words, but I speak the truth. Let him run with the Pack. I myself will teach him."

"We need yet another," said Akela. "Who speaks besides Baloo?"

An inky shadow silently dropped down into the circle. Bagheera, the Black Panther, turned to face Akela.

Everyone knew Bagheera. And no one cared to cross his path. He was as cunning as a jackal, as bold as a buffalo, and as reckless as a wounded elephant. Yet he had a voice as soft as honey and skin as sleek as silk.

"O Akela, and you the Free People," he purred. "I know I have no right to be at Pack Council. But the Law of the Jungle says that if there is doubt about a cub, its life may be bought at a price. And the Law does not say who may or may not pay that price. Am I right?"

Akela merely nodded.

"Now to Baloo's word," Bagheera continued, "I will add one newly killed bull, not half a mile away, if you accept the man's cub. Is it a bargain?"

"Good! Good!" clamored the young wolves, who were always hungry. "What matter? He will die in the winter rains. He will scorch in the sun. What harm can he do us? Where is the bull, Bagheera? Let the man-cub be accepted." Then came Akela's deep cry, "Look well! Look well, O Wolves!"

Mowgli was still playing with the pebbles. He didn't notice as the wolves came and looked at him one by one. At last the wolves went down the hill. Only Akela, Bagheera, Baloo, and Mowgli's own wolves stayed behind. Shere Khan still roared in the night, for he was angry that Mowgli hadn't been handed over to him.

"Yes, roar well," said Bagheera, almost to himself. "The time will come when this boy will make you roar another tune."

Now you must be content to skip ten or eleven whole years and only guess at the wonderful life Mowgli led with the wolves. If it were written out it would fill far more than one book. He grew up with the cubs, and Father Wolf taught him his business. Every rustle in the grass, every breath of night air, and every note of the owls became a familiar friend.

But his most important teacher was Baloo, the wise old brown bear. Mowgli was a fast pupil, and Baloo taught him well. By this time, the boy could climb as well as he could swim. And he swam almost as well as he could run. So Baloo taught him the Wood and Water Laws, and even the Strangers' Hunting Call.

When he was not learning, Mowgli sat out in the sun and slept. When he felt dirty or hot, he swam in the forest pools. When he wanted honey or nuts, he climbed up for them, as Bagheera taught him. He took his place at the Council Rock, too. He discovered that if he stared hard at any wolf, the wolf was forced to drop his eyes. Sometimes Mowgli stared just for fun.

At other times he would pick the long thorns out of the pads of his friends' feet. He would go down into the farmlands at night, and look curiously at the villagers in their huts. But Mowgli had a distrust of people. Bagheera had shown him a box with a drop gate so cunningly hidden in the jungle that he nearly walked into it. Bagheera had warned him that it was a trap.

By this time, Akela was a very old wolf. Many of the
younger wolves had begun to drift away from the ways
of the Pack. They followed Shere Khan, and fed on his
leftovers. And the tiger was beginning to turn some of
them against Mowgli.

Mother Wolf told Mowgli that Shere Khan was not to
be trusted, and that some day he must kill the tiger.
A young wolf would have remembered that advice, but
Mowgli forgot it because he was only a boy. Though,
of course, he would have called himself a wolf if he could
speak in any human language.

One day Bagheera came lounging through the jungle to
see how Mowgli's lessons were progressing. He purred
with his head against a tree as the boy recited the Law.

''Tell Bagheera the Master Words of the Jungle that
I've taught you today,'' said Baloo.

''Master Words for which people?'' asked Mowgli,
delighted to show off. ''The Jungle has many
tongues. *I* know them all.''

"You know a little, but not much," said Baloo. "See, Bagheera, they never thank their teacher. Say the Word for the Hunting People then—great scholar."

"We be of one blood, you and I," said Mowgli, giving the words the Bear accent which all the Hunting People use. Then he used the Bird and the Snake accents, ending with a perfectly indescribable hiss.

"With those words, the boy need fear no one," Baloo

said, patting his furry stomach with pride.

"Except his own tribe," said Bagheera. "Watch out for my ribs, Little Brother! What is all this jumping up and down?"

Mowgli had climbed onto Bagheera's back, where he sat sideways, drumming his heels on the glossy skin. "And so I shall have a tribe of my own," he shouted. "And lead them through the branches all day long!"

"What is this new foolishness?" asked Bagheera.

"They have promised me this. Ah!"

Whoof! Baloo's giant paw scooped Mowgli off Bagheera's back. As the boy lay between the big forepaws, he could see Baloo was angry. He looked at Bagheera to see if he was angry too. The panther's eyes were as hard as jade stones.

"You've been with the Monkey People? The people without a law?"

"They came down from the trees and gave me nuts and good things to eat," Mowgli protested. "And they carried me up between the branches. They said I was their blood brother and should be their leader some day."

"They have *no* leader," said Bagheera. "They lied. They always lie."

"They boast and chatter and pretend that they're a great people," Baloo added. "Then the falling of a leaf turns their heads and their plans are forgotten."

A shower of sticks and nuts suddenly rained down on the heads of the three. The next thing Mowgli knew, a dozen hands were grabbing at him, pulling him up into the trees. Baloo roared, and Bagheera sprang upward, but there was little they could do. Mowgli had been taken prisoner by the Monkey People—the *Bandar-log*!

Bounding and crashing and whooping and yelling, the tribe of *Bandar-log* swept through the trees. Two of the strongest swung Mowgli through the branches, twenty feet at a bound. The glimpses of the earth far below frightened him.

Mowgli knew that at the pace the monkeys were going, Baloo and Bagheera would soon be left far behind. He grew angry, and began to think. Then he saw, far away in the blue, Chil the Kite balancing and wheeling through the sky.

The bird wasn't having much luck with his afternoon's hunting. When he saw the monkeys carrying something, Chil flew closer to see if it was something good to eat. He whistled with surprise when he saw Mowgli being dragged up to a treetop. He was even more surprised to hear him give the Bird call for "We be of one blood, you and I."

"Mark my trail," Mowgli shouted. "Tell Baloo and Bagheera!"

Chil nodded, for none of the Jungle People could ignore the Master Words. He flew up till he looked no bigger than a speck of dust. He rocked on his wings, his feet gathered under him, and watched as the *Bandar-log* whirled along.

Meanwhile, Baloo and Bagheera were furious. The panther had chased the monkeys halfway up the tree after Mowgli. But the thin upper branches broke beneath his weight. He slipped down the trunk, his claws full of bark.

"The Monkey People have no reason to fear us," said Bagheera, licking one forepaw thoughtfully. "They know we can't follow them a hundred feet above ground."

"But there is one they *do* fear," said Baloo. "Kaa the Rock Snake. He can climb trees as well as they can."

They found the big python stretched out on a warm rock ledge in the afternoon sun. "Good hunting!" cried Baloo. It was the greeting the Jungle People used when they met one another in passing.

"Good hunting for us all," hissed Kaa. "One of us at least is hungry."

"We are hunting," said Baloo carelessly. He knew you mustn't hurry Kaa.

"Let me come with you," said Kaa. "A blow more or less is nothing to you. I have to climb in the trees half the night, and the branches are not what they used to be. I nearly fell on my last hunt. The noise of my slipping woke up the *Bandar-log,* and they called me most evil names."

"Footless, yellow earthworm," said Bagheera softly, as if he were trying to remember something.

"Sssss! Have they ever called me *that?*" asked a very angry Kaa.

"Something of the sort," the panther answered.

"It's the *Bandar-log* we're following now," said Baloo. "They have stolen our man-cub. And we know that of all the Jungle People, they fear Kaa alone."

"They have good reason," Kaa replied, twisting his thirty-foot body into fantastic coils and curves. "Perhaps they need to be reminded."

"Up, up! Hello, hello!" came a voice from above. Baloo looked up to see Chil the Kite circling overhead.

"I've seen Mowgli among the *Bandar-log*," cried Chil. "They've taken him beyond the river to the monkey city, the Cold Lairs. He asked me to tell you."

"Come! We must go quickly," said Bagheera. "It's half a night's journey, at full speed." He eyed Baloo cautiously. The lumbering old brown bear looked serious.

"I'll go as fast as I can," he said.

"It won't be fast enough," Bagheera said simply. "Kaa and I will go ahead. Follow!"

In the Cold Lairs, the Monkey People were not thinking of Mowgli's friends at all. They had taken him to their Lost City, an abandoned palace built by some long-forgotten king. Mowgli had never seen an Indian city before. Though this one was in ruins, it must once have been magnificent.

Twenty or thirty monkeys bounded away to get Mowgli some fruit and nuts. But they fell to fighting on the road, and it was too much trouble to go back for the food. Sore and angry as well as hungry, Mowgli watched the tribe gather in small groups. Their behavior thoroughly confused him.

Instead of going to sleep, as Mowgli would have done, the *Bandar-log* joined hands and danced about and sang foolish songs. They sang of how wise and good and clever and strong they were. Then they made speeches about the great plans they would make. Mowgli suspected (and rightly so) that none of those plans would ever amount to anything.

"We are the most wonderful people in the jungle," the monkeys shouted. "We all say so, and so it must be true."

Through it all, Mowgli roamed through the empty city, giving the Strangers' Hunting Call from time to time. No one answered. "Baloo was right," he thought to himself. "These people have no Law, no Hunting Call, no leader. If I'm starved or killed here, it's all my fault. I must try to get back to my own jungle." But every time he reached the city walls, the monkeys pulled him back.

They led him to a terrace near some red sandstone water tanks, half-filled with rain. On one side stood a building that used to serve as the queen's summer house.

By now it was very late. Mowgli watched as a cloud began to cover the moon. "If it were a big enough cloud, I might try to run away in the darkness," Mowgli thought. "But I'm far too tired."

Yet even as he lay down and began to drift asleep, he could hear the dancing, laughing monkeys all around him.

"We are great. We are wonderful. We will tell you all about our excellent selves!"

That same cloud Mowgli saw was being watched by two good friends in a ditch below the city wall. Bagheera and Kaa, knowing how dangerous the Monkey People were in large numbers, did not take any risks.

"I will go to the west wall," whispered Kaa. "From there I can come down swiftly, with the slope of the ground in my favor. They won't jump on *my* back by the hundreds, but—"

"I know it," Bagheera answered.

When the cloud covered the moon completely, Bagheera crept to the terrace. The big cat raced up the slope almost without a sound. A circle of fifty or sixty monkeys had gathered around Mowgli. Bagheera struck, left and right, as Mowgli woke up with a start.

The monkeys howled in fright and rage. But as Bagheera tripped on the rolling, kicking bodies beneath him, he heard one shout, "There is only one! Get him!"

A scuffling mass of monkeys closed over Bagheera. Five or six held on to Mowgli and dragged him to the summer house, pushing him through a hole in its broken dome. An ordinary boy would have been badly bruised, but Mowgli fell as Baloo had taught him. He landed perfectly on his feet.

Mowgli looked out through a grating and listened to the yells and chatterings and scufflings of the struggle. He heard Bagheera's deep, hoarse cough as the panther twisted and plunged under his enemies.

"Baloo must be nearby. Bagheera would not have come alone," thought Mowgli. Then he called aloud, "To the tanks, Bagheera. Roll to the water tanks. They won't follow you in the water."

Bagheera heard, and the cry that told him Mowgli was safe gave him new courage. He worked his way, inch by inch, to the water tanks. Then from the ruined wall nearest the jungle came the rumbling war cry of Baloo.

The old bear panted up the terrace only to disappear up to the head in a wave of monkeys. Spreading out his forepaws, he began to strike out with a regular *bat-bat-bat*, like the flipping strokes of a paddle wheel. A crash and a splash told Mowgli that Bagheera had finally reached the water tanks.

Kaa had only just worked his way over the wall. He came straight, quickly, toward the heart of the crowd around Baloo.

Now, the fighting strength of a python is in the driving blow of its head, backed by the weight of its body. If you can imagine a battering ram weighing half a ton, you can imagine what Kaa was like when he fought. One blow was all it took to scatter the monkeys in panic. "Kaa!" they screamed. "It's Kaa! Run! Run!"

Then Kaa opened his mouth and spoke one long, hissing word. The faraway monkeys, hurrying to the safety of the Cold Lairs, stayed where they were. In the stillness that fell, Mowgli heard Bagheera shaking his wet sides as he came up from the tank. "Get the man-cub out of that trap," he said. "I can do no more. Let's take him and go. They may attack again."

"They won't move until I order them," hissed Kaa.

"I'm not sure they didn't pull me into a hundred little bearlings," said Baloo, gravely shaking one leg after the other.

"Stand back, manling, I will break down the wall."

The python sent half a dozen full-power smashing blows into the wall. It fell in a cloud of dust and rubbish. Mowgli leaped through the opening and flung himself between Baloo and Bagheera, an arm around each neck.

"And here is Kaa, to whom we owe the battle and you owe your life," said Bagheera. "Thank him according to our customs, Mowgli."

"We be of one blood, you and I," Mowgli answered. "I take my life from you tonight. My hunt shall be your hunt if ever you are hungry, O Kaa."

The python dropped his head for a moment on Mowgli's shoulder. "A brave heart and a courteous tongue," he said. "That will carry you far through the jungle. But go now. The moon sets."

"Yes. That's more than enough for one night," Bagheera agreed. "Jump on my back, Little Brother, and let's go home."

On a very warm day some weeks later, Mowgli lay sleepily in the jungle with his head on Bagheera's glossy black skin.

"Little Brother," the Panther asked seriously, "how often have I told you that Shere Khan is your enemy?"

"As many times as there are nuts on that palm," said Mowgli, who, naturally, could not count. "What of it? The tiger is all long tail and loud talk, like Mor the Peacock."

"Open those eyes, Little Brother," Bagheera said. "Shere Khan won't dare kill you in the jungle. But remember, Akela is very old. Soon the day will come when he can no longer hunt, and then he will be leader no more. Many of the wolves that looked you over when you were brought to Council are old too. The young ones believe, as Shere Khan has taught them, that a man-cub has no place in the Pack. And soon you will be a man."

"I was born in the jungle," Mowgli said angrily. "I have obeyed the Law of the Jungle. There is no wolf of ours from whose paws I haven't pulled thorns. Surely they're my brothers and sisters!"

"By your very carelessness they know you are a man," Bagheera continued. "Not even I, the Black Panther, can look you between the eyes. The others hate you because their eyes can't meet yours, because you've pulled thorns from their feet—because you are a man.

"When Akela misses his next kill, the Pack will turn against him. And against you. And then—and then— I have it!"

Bagheera leaped to his feet. "Go down to the village and take some of the Red Flower that they grow there in pots. It will be an even stronger friend than Bagheera or Baloo or those of the Pack that trust you."

By the Red Flower Bagheera meant fire, but the Jungle People avoid calling fire by its real name. They live in deadly fear of it, and invent a hundred ways of describing it.

"I'll go," said Mowgli. "But are you sure, Bagheera? Are you sure that all this is Shere Khan's doing?"

"Absolutely."

"Then, by the Bull that bought me, I will make him pay for this," said Mowgli, as he bounded away.

"That is a man. That is all a man," said Bagheera to himself, lying down again. "Oh, Shere Khan. There was never a blacker hunting than your man-cub hunt ten years ago."

Mowgli plunged through the bushes to the stream at the bottom of the valley. There he stopped, for he heard the yell of the Pack hunting. A hunted buck bellowed, then snorted as it turned at bay. There were wicked, bitter howls from the young wolves. "Akela! Akela! Let the Lone Wolf show his strength. Room for the leader of the Pack! Spring, Akela!"

Akela must have sprung and missed. Mowgli heard the snap of his teeth and then a yelp as the buck knocked the wolf over with his forefoot.

Mowgli didn't wait for anything more. He went on to the village and found the Red Flower growing in a wicker pot plastered inside with earth. "Bagheera was right," he thought. "Tomorrow will be a day for both Akela and me."

All through the next day, Mowgli tended the fire as he had seen the villagers do. That evening, one of the young wolves came and told him rudely that he was wanted on the Council Rock. Mowgli laughed until the animal ran away. Then he went to the Council, still laughing.

Akela lay by the side of his rock as a sign that the leadership of the Pack was open. Shere Khan walked to and fro, being flattered by his following of scrap-fed wolves. The tiger began to speak—something he would never have dared to do when Akela was in his prime.

Mowgli sprang to his feet. "Free People," he cried, "does Shere Khan lead the Pack? What does a tiger have to do with our leadership?"

"What have we to do with this toothless fool?" Shere Khan roared, looking at Akela. "It is the man-cub who has lived too long. Give him to me!"

More than half the pack began to yell. "A man! A man! What has a man to do with us? Let him go to his own place."

Then Mowgli stood up, with the fire pot in his hands. "Listen, you dogs," he said. "You've told me so often that I am a man that I feel your words are true. So I do not call you my brothers and sisters anymore, but *dogs*, as a man should."

He flung the fire pot on the ground. Some of the red coals lit a tuft of dried moss that flared up. All the Council drew back from the flames in terror.

Mowgli thrust a dead branch into the fire. "Good!" he said. "I see that you are dogs. I go from you to my own people."

Mowgli walked to where Shere Khan sat blinking stupidly at the flames, and held the branch under the tiger's chin. "Up, dog!" he cried. "Up, when a man speaks, or I will set your coat on fire." Shere Khan whimpered and whined with fear, but obeyed.

Mowgli held the branch high, and swung it right and left around the circle of wolves. They ran howling with the sparks burning their fur.

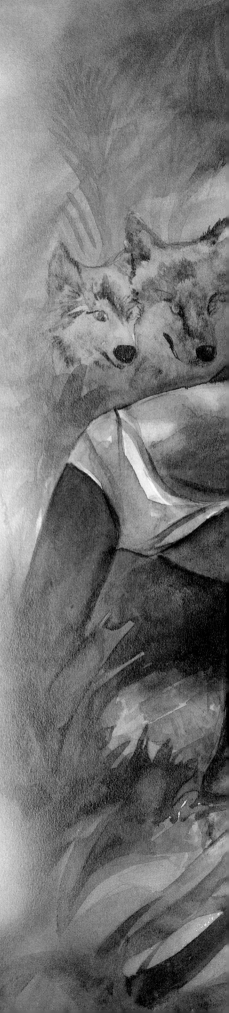

The Council over, Mowgli went to the cave where Mother and Father Wolf lived. He cried on Mother Wolf's coat while the four cubs howled miserably.

"Promise you won't forget me?" he asked.

"Not while we can follow a trail," said Gray Brother, the oldest of the cubs. "Come to the foot of the hill by night, and we'll talk with you there."

"Come soon!" said Father Wolf. "For we are old, your mother and I."

"I will surely come," Mowgli promised. "And when I do, it will be to lay out Shere Khan's hide on the Council Rock."

The dawn was beginning to break when Mowgli went down the hillside alone, to meet those mysterious things called humans.

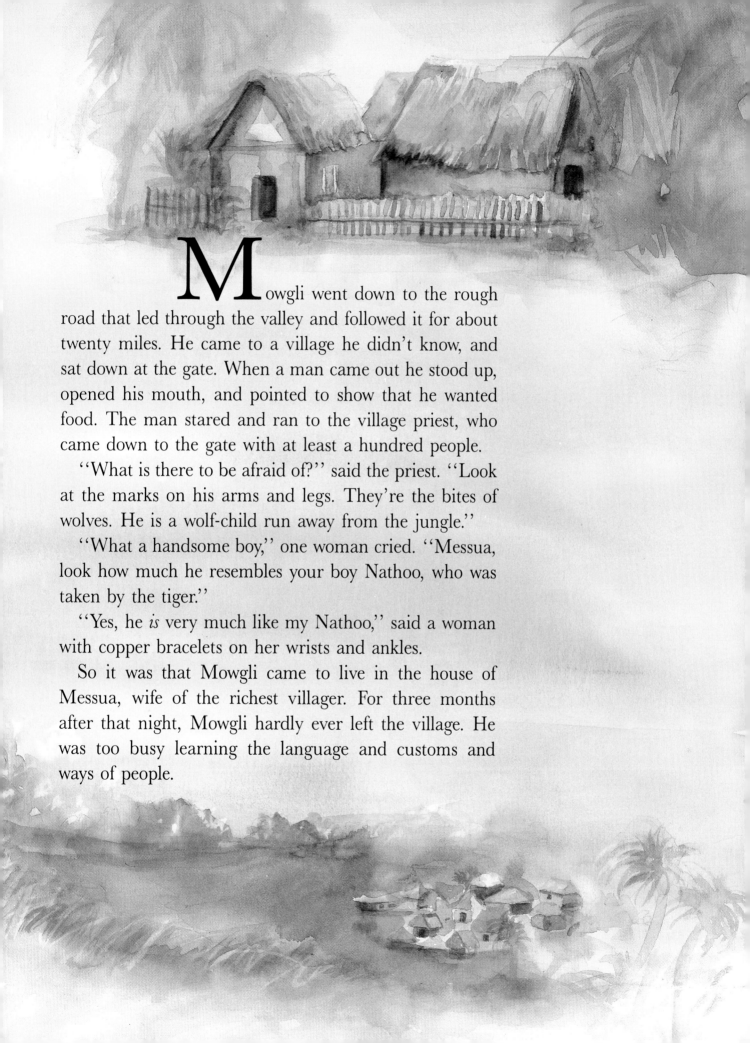

Mowgli went down to the rough road that led through the valley and followed it for about twenty miles. He came to a village he didn't know, and sat down at the gate. When a man came out he stood up, opened his mouth, and pointed to show that he wanted food. The man stared and ran to the village priest, who came down to the gate with at least a hundred people.

"What is there to be afraid of?" said the priest. "Look at the marks on his arms and legs. They're the bites of wolves. He is a wolf-child run away from the jungle."

"What a handsome boy," one woman cried. "Messua, look how much he resembles your boy Nathoo, who was taken by the tiger."

"Yes, he *is* very much like my Nathoo," said a woman with copper bracelets on her wrists and ankles.

So it was that Mowgli came to live in the house of Messua, wife of the richest villager. For three months after that night, Mowgli hardly ever left the village. He was too busy learning the language and customs and ways of people.

In the evenings, he often sat with the men in the village club, a platform built under a great fig tree. They told wonderful tales of gods and heroes and ghosts. Buldeo, the village hunter, told even more wonderful ones about the jungle.

But sometimes Mowgli had to cover his face to hide his laughter while Buldeo spun his stories. Once Buldeo claimed that Shere Khan was a ghost-tiger—the spirit of an old moneylender who had died years ago. "I know this is true," he said, "because the moneylender always walked with a limp, and this tiger limps too!"

"Are all these tales such cobwebs and moon talk?" Mowgli interrupted. "The tiger limps because he was born lame, as everyone knows."

Buldeo was speechless for a moment. Then he said, "If you are so wise, bring his hide to the government. They have a reward of a hundred rupees on his head. Better still, don't talk when your elders speak."

"It's time that boy went into herding," said the cattle-master. "That will teach him some responsibility."

Mowgli was told to take the village cattle and buffaloes out to the fields with the other herd boys. Riding on the back of Rama, the great lead bull, he guided the animals with a long, polished bamboo stick. He would take the buffaloes to the river, then trot off to a small clump of bamboo to meet Gray Brother. Here he could get word on the news of the jungle—and of Shere Khan.

"He's come back to this territory," Gray Brother said one day. "He means to wait for you at the village gate this evening. For you and no one else. He's sleeping now in a ravine nearby. He hunted at dawn and has eaten well."

"The fool! Does he think I'll wait till he has slept?" Mowgli asked in disgust. "I could take the buffalo herd to the head of the ravine and then sweep down, but he would slink out at the foot. Gray Brother, can you cut the herd in two?"

"Not I perhaps. But I have brought a wise helper." Gray Brother trotted off a short way. Then a huge gray head that Mowgli knew well rose from the undergrowth.

"Akela!" Mowgli laughed, clapping his hands. "I might have known that you wouldn't forget me."

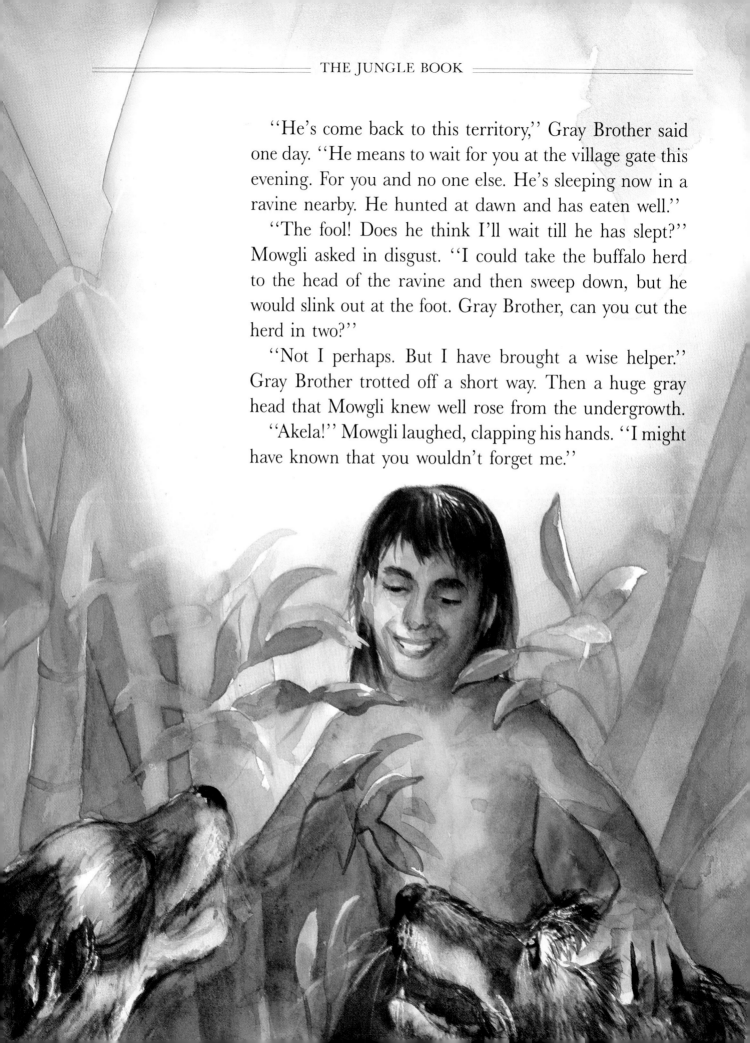

The two wolves ran in and out of the herd, moving the bulls to one side and the calves and cows to the other. Mowgli slipped onto Rama's back. "Gray Brother, hold the cows together and drive them into the foot of the ravine," he shouted. "Keep them there till we come down."

The bulls swept off as Akela bayed. "Turn them, Akela. Turn them quickly," cried Mowgli. "Rama is mad with rage. If I could only tell him what I need of him today! But I don't speak his language."

The bulls crashed into the standing thicket. Akela had dropped far behind, only growling once or twice to hurry the rear guard. It was a long, long circle. If they got too near the sides of the ravine, their scent would give Shere Khan warning.

When they reached the head of the ravine, Mowgli looked down its steep walls, covered with vines and creepers. Those walls would offer no foothold for a tiger who wanted to get out.

41

Mowgli put his hands to his mouth and shouted, and the echoes jumped from rock to rock. After a long time there came back the drawling, sleepy snarl of a full-fed tiger just wakened.

"Who calls?" asked Shere Khan.

"I, Mowgli. It's time to come to the Council Rock. Hurry them down, Akela! Down, Rama, down!"

The herd pitched over the edge of the slope, one after the other. Sand and stones spurted up around them. Once started, there was no chance of stopping. When they were barely at the bottom, Rama caught Shere Khan's scent and bellowed.

The torrent of black horns, foaming muzzles, and staring eyes whirled down the ravine just as the boulders go down it in floodtime. Shere Khan heard the thunder of their hoofs and lumbered away, looking for some way to escape. There was none.

The herd splashed through the pool the tiger had just left, bellowing till the walls rang. Mowgli heard an answering bellow from down below. Gray Brother had done his job with the rest of the herd.

Shere Khan turned. He knew if it came to the worst, it was better to face the bulls than the cows with their calves. Then Rama tripped, and with the bulls at his heels, crashed full into the other herd. The weaker buffaloes were lifted clean off their feet by the shock.

Akela and Gray Brother ran left and right, nipping at the buffaloes' heels to break up the herd and keep them from fighting. Mowgli managed to turn Rama, and the others followed him to the river.

The buffaloes had earned their rest, and Shere Khan needed no more trampling. Mowgli's enemy was dead.

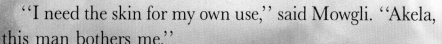

Brothers, that was a dog's death,"
said Mowgli, feeling for the knife he always carried now
that he lived with people. "His hide would look well on
the Council Rock. We must get to work right away."

Suddenly, a hand fell on his shoulder. Looking up he
saw Buldeo, carrying his musket. The other herd boys
had run back to the village when they saw the buffaloes
stampede. Buldeo had come, eager to correct Mowgli for
not taking better care of the herd. The wolves dropped
out of sight as soon as they saw him.

"You fool!" Buldeo laughed. "You think you can skin
a tiger? The lame tiger too, and there is a hundred rupees
on his head. Well, well, perhaps I'll give you one of the
rupees when I've taken the skin to the government office."

"I need the skin for my own use," said Mowgli. "Akela,
this man bothers me."

Buldeo found himself sprawled on the grass with a gray wolf standing over him. Mowgli set about his work as if he were alone in all of India.

"Ye-es," he said, between his teeth. "There is an old war between this lame tiger and myself. A very old war. And I have won."

To be fair to Buldeo, if he had been ten years younger he would have taken his chance with Akela if he'd met the wolf in the woods. But a wolf who obeyed the orders of this boy who had private wars with man-eating tigers was not a common animal. It was sorcery of the worst kind.

"O Great King," he said at last in a husky whisper. "I am an old man. I didn't know that you were anything other than a herd boy. May I get up and go away, or will your servant tear me to pieces?"

Mowgli nodded to Akela, and the wolf let Buldeo go. The hunter went back to the village as fast as he could. There, he told the excited crowd a tale of magic and enchantment and sorcery that made the priest look very serious.

When Mowgli finally finished his work, it was nearly dark. He said to the wolves, "Now we must hide the skin and take the buffaloes back to the village. Come."

At the village gate, Mowgli saw lights and heard the temple bells clanging. Half the village seemed to be waiting by the gate. Then a shower of stones whistled about his ears. "Sorcerer! Wolf's brat!" the villagers shouted. "Go away! Shoot, Buldeo!"

"Now what is this?" asked Mowgli, as Buldeo's musket fired.

"They're not unlike the Pack, these brothers of yours," Akela observed, sitting down calmly. "It would seem that, if bullets mean anything, they want to cast you out."

"Again? Last time it was because I was a man. This time it's because I am a wolf!" Mowgli replied. "Let's go, Akela. Come, Gray Brother."

A woman ran out of the crowd. It was Messua. "My son!" she sobbed. "They say you are a wizard who can turn into a beast at will. I don't believe them, but go away or they will kill you."

"I am no wizard, Messua," Mowgli called back. "Farewell!"

When the moon rose, the villagers saw Mowgli, with two wolves at his heels and a bundle on his head, trotting across the plain. It would be morning before the three would reach the cave Mowgli used to call home.

Thy cast me out of the Man Pack, Mother," Mowgli said to Mother Wolf. "But I come with the hide of Shere Khan to keep my word."

Old Mother Wolf walked stiffly out of the cave. When she saw the tiger skin, her eyes glowed.

Mowgli, Akela, and Gray Brother ran up to the Council Rock together. Mowgli spread the skin out over the flat stone where Akela used to sit. Akela lay down across it and called out the old call to the Council, "Look, look well, O Wolves!"

Ever since Akela had been forced to step down, the Pack had been without a leader. Still, they answered his call from habit, and saw Shere Khan's striped hide on the rock.

"Look well, O Wolves. Have I not kept my word?" said Mowgli.

"Well done, Little Brother," purred a deep, throaty voice. Bagheera gazed at the Council Rock approvingly. "Now all the Jungle People may rest easier. With the cattle-killer gone, we've made peace with the villagers at last."

"Not I," said Mowgli bitterly. "Man Pack and Wolf Pack have cast me out. Now I will hunt alone."

"We'll hunt with you," said the four wolf cubs.

So Mowgli went away and hunted with the cubs in the
jungle from that day on. He was not always alone, because,
years afterward, he became a man and married.
But that is a story for grownups.